Into the Blue

– the journey continues –

Other Books by Fred K. Taylor

Ask No Questions
Poems and Stories

Unpredictable Outcomes
A Military Memoir from Blue Water Navy to Red Mud Seabees

Contributed to:
Five Poets Write About Aging, Illness, and Mortality

Into the Blue

– the journey continues –

Fred K. Taylor

IMAGO
PRESS

TUCSON ARIZONA

Published in the United States of America by:

Pennywyse Press
3710 East Edison Street
Tucson, AZ 85716

Library of Congress Control Number: 2014933640

ISBN 978-1-935437-87-1
ISBN 1-935437-87-9

Book and Cover Design by Leila Joiner
All interior illustrations and cover art © Fred K. Taylor

Printed in the United States of America on Acid-Free Paper

To my sister, Cindy, who typed most of what makes up this book and for being patient with me in her efforts to read my poor writing. Thanks for all you do.

Table of Contents

Poems

Stories

Blue

Blue, dark, light, whatever is in-between. All blue until without notice you're in a blue-green. There is a long list of proper names for all the colors I see spreading all about, but I don't know the proper names. I just know it's a world of blues and in unexpected places, blue-green.

I travel through these colors, slipping from shade to shade until suddenly a red. A long line of red, thin on the ends and thicker in the middle, and then on the edge a weak orange.

This is different. It gives the world a point of reference. Just so far from the red to your left, reference. A comfortable world of blends and shades with an unsteady line of red, no real form just red. Then the world changes in great detail relatively speaking. A flower is found with three colors, brown, yellow and green. Now we have form, purpose and structure in a world of blends. This is the center of everything; our newfound focus, "the flower."

Stand aside the many, the blue that goes on forever in shades of light, dark, and in between. Then the blue-greens you cover great areas, but count for little when compared to "the flower." This is the way of people and how they look at things.

Poems

Acrylic State of Mind

Doesn't it always happen
When I am in an acrylic state of mind
Watercolor paper is all that can be found

Some days it goes the other way
Watercolor ideas
But canvas is all that I can put my hands on
So now you know
The inventory blues
Seen from a right brain view.

Or when you have magic in your hand
With perfect picture in the head
Quickly take paper and pencil to hand
Progress stops
The pencil point is down to wood
The moment passed
Magic gone
So shop a lot
Buy right
Don't lose the magic
Be ready
Every day
When a moment happens
Grab it
With perfect brush at hand.

After All These Years

The two of us on the road
With 20 years on the farm
Changes come fast on the road
Read the sign quick
Know when to keep moving and when to rest
Look out for weather
Know the limits of body and vehicle
500 miles a day all the old bones can do on a good road or not
Rest stops take on a whole new meaning
The mind might be willing but the bladder is full.

I sit in the back seat
You the driver
For days I see only the back of your head or your face in the mirror
Not the entire face just the tired eyes watching the road
Hour after hour I want it to be as before
You and me face to face.

There are miles to go before we rest tonight
There are many sights
The wild deer, the western antelope, the Midwestern beef cattle
All feeding on the sea of grassland for hundreds of miles
Long trains do impress
Rough roads not
On the high plains the sky is big but color is not
Road noise at 75 mph
Wind rushing by
Tires humming across the road.

It's a big country for two old homebodies
On the road again.

An Important Event

It was an important event
Time lost in the moments of our personal history
Sitting around the office table signing property deeds and
important stuff
Buying a most expensive house
Serious business
Intense concentration on all four faces
Fred not feeling well
Faye watching over all his needs
Time went on
Its endless linear path and still we had the big money check
Then a bug started flying around becoming a pest
A bigger and bigger pest
It bothered Fred twice
Which sealed its doom
For then the bug landed on the conference table
In front of all
Quick as a wild cat's paw
Faye's hand strikes
A loud bang echoes through the office
People jump and turn
It was a true and heavy strike
The bug is dead.

People stare, eyes wide, mouths open
Then recover speech making comments
"That was fast"
"No hesitation"
"Let me get you a tissue."

Fred looks at Faye with pride
Thinking that's how a Wisconsin farm girl gets things done.

Art in the Sun

Before my afternoon nap, glancing out the window, I see quite a sight. Despite the bright sunlight, round bales in the field, some tilting left there. And there leaning right to the right of the tilting left bale is another. Some not standing at all, but all wound tight showing green fading to brown and gold. So different this looks from a few days ago. This hillside field with tree-lined borders is now a living canvas of great size. The tree line has become the art exhibit of "round bales in the sun;" it's not just hay anymore. Their placement on the slope makes one think of why there and not elsewhere, or what's the pattern? All this with a background of bird songs. What an opening day, but now it's time to stop. For this poem just landed in my lap, now I take my nap.

Art Show

The carpet short
A pale green with a slight feeling of blue
Colors that fit an art show
My head bent down
Muscles twisted to the right
I see more of this rug than most
Due to this special point of view
Rug which carries many
Counts the passing of their feet
Feet that tread heavy and light
Yet quiet considering the numbers
A carpet soft to the step
No one slips
And few even think of what is under foot
Across the room to the east
Leaving the solid support of rug and floor
A large window frames an impressive view
Green palms sharp and bold with a background of purple
Undefined mountains causing one to wonder
If the eastern sky is now filled with dark storm clouds
Wind moving everything
A wild mix to tease the mind
Turning focus from point to point
Sound fills the room
Close the eyes and it becomes almost too much
A jazzy bass commands some level of my body
The Parkinson's tremor barely can resist joining
In some wild moving event
Add a background sound
What seems a hundred times a hundred voices, all talking
The level has me searching for my thoughts
Found hiding at times from the mad tempest
This so completely opposite from the quiet of home
Here the pace is fast
I stand aside to survive.

Artist Expectations

Artist Expectations fill the air
Thick and varied
On this the first day of the Saddlebrooke
Very fine, not craft art show
Untrained but showing I sit in a crowd of people
Yet apart in my thoughts
Silently thinking, verbalizing sparingly
Dusting off little used skills
Cannot have the stiff expression that does not sell art
Or bring a second look.

My weather eye watching
The wind that can blow the goods quick to the ground
It is a pleasant place
Live oak in southwest courtyard
Nearby stream and pines
Make a beautiful backdrop
The sun bright almost hot on football Saturday
Badgers versus 'Nitty Lions
People come and look
Old bones assemblage not sold
But cut loose one old crone.

A good day for first day
Business and social
Took some effort
Day ended fast
Closed at four to find the Badgers had lost
And some art sells.

Big Blue Bird

I am not a big blue bird
I don't fly where I want
I buy tickets on Midwest Express
Thought it was best
Now no first class on Midwest
Legs that need room find no comfort
Removing the sock does it help?
Dwell on the aches until man with no arm passes by
His smile puts my aches in their place
Still it has to be said
We are packed like corks in a bottle
So tight all I can do is wiggle my toes
Down the narrow aisle a little boy passes
I think of my youth
Am I flying back in time to my boyhood past?
Might I reach the past unable to hear?
Don't remember planes being so noisy
We are both getting old
The plane and I
If the uncomfortable feet would let me
I would fall to sleep
To free the mind from the present
To find a pleasant place
To wake in some yet to be tomorrow
We still fly on
Starving for space
I think how soon
I come to miss the comfort of home
With no crowds in my house
Not like today in the clouds
A hundred eyes close by
Pressing in a little space
Now I notice on the wall
A thread bare cloth

I read "the best care in the air."
 The cloth is fading, as is the message
A message from a different day.

Choked

Silently I choked
No words came through
Wounded participles
And fractured nouns
Some of the casualties of my stories and verse
The battlefields of my literary efforts
Had, will have, has many victims
Being somewhat impervious to good grammar and her kin
I keep pen in hand and paper close.

Comfort

Comfort, where do you find it?
When the body has so many aches, shakes and pains
When sleep comes hard or not at all
Given all the chokes, gasps and coughs
It's hard to find a position with any comfort and still breathe
Simple things are hard to do when the left side has Parkinson's
Add a swollen hand black and blue with a broken finger too!
Nothing is warm enough
I have the chills
Minutes pass
I'm so hot with fever, sweats
Pills I take so many just to reach this level of comfort
Pills big and small, all different colors
Some you dare not forget, others you better not forget
Take some with food, others not
The side effects are many
Let's not talk of that
Cough so hard I can't hear myself think
But then for a moment a short but very clear day dream.

It was quiet
I could lie still with no discomfort
Breathing not a problem
No trouble to move or to reach or use my hands
Not too hot or too cool
Pill taking? I don't have to worry.

What's this?
I don't feel the passing of time!
You're not here
So that would be time apart from you
No! I want my time
Life is not easy or simple
Comfort where do you find it?

Does one want to pay the cost?
No, not today.

Contest Rules

Contest rules!
Not great news for contest rules, not your way
Applies to you and you and maybe you
The kept poet of the keep
I know your face
You look like an entry form
Turn forms in at the proper date
In, on or before a postmark at midnight
No entry fee
But send money to the address on the back
Money or poems will not be returned
If you lose or win
The category that can't be found must be completed in full
And not returned
Contestants may enter one or less than one entry
Those must be placed on an odd piece of paper made by hand
Give us notification when name does not appear very clear
Prizes will be awarded to all contest judges
Need to call for awards
Unlisted number not listed
Remember
Contest rules or disqualification blues.

Corner Seat

I sit in my corner seat out of the way next to the stone fireplace
Room full of many feet
I watch the floor and witness the passing shoes
Big shoes and little shoes, old leather, plastic and rubber
Open toed and many, many tennis shoes
Old style, new style, then some very new
The very best spit and polished dress shoes
Soon followed the simple as can be bare feet
Then came wrapped in leather sandals the tattooed foot
Making a statement
All moving to some unheard music in a strange unexplained dance
Fast feet mixing with slow
Pointing this way and that
Then they all move to another spot
Every kind of shoe and foot
Moving to and fro is how I see the art show.

Sitting in my chair
The hours pass at the show
Heavy head bent low
Get to see a lot of the floor
Look up, meet the faces, say hellos
But wild imagination and slow business
Start my daydreams
I see in my mind
Myself walking plowed
Wisconsin farm fields
Arrowheads in my thoughts
Searching for pieces from the past
Fresh wind blows
The sky clear and blue and then I hear
"Return! Return!"
"Social control to day dream, social control to day dream."
"Attention to the here and now."

"You're at an art show. People are talking to you."
"Social demands demand attention."

Imagination can play another day, but not today.

Creative Costs

Yet to be found
Writer dutifully lives at a Hollywood address
Artsy hole in the wall
Falls to sleep in a crowded corner
Laptop running and ready
For the next story line found in her dreams
Lives the plots in her mind.

Short nights end
Day job calls its demands at morning light
Doesn't the body call for more comfort?

Thirty something going on forty
The industry must have a great draw
The undiscovered writers give it their all
They mortgage their tomorrows for the maybe screen plays to be
Comfort and security go lacking for the possible Hollywood payoff.

Does this compare to the brushstroke dreams of the artist?
Painting their dreams in exchange for material comfort
Driven to seek their success in colors, shapes and forms
To feel the intensity of the project's focus
Give up much for the pursuit
Is this the nature of the beast of artful fulfillment?
Can there be a balance?

Day Break

Day break, dawns light
Faye wakes
Sleepy head
We get out of bed
Soon we talk
Start the day
At dawns faint light
Listen to the departure of the night
Going from the light
Hello good morning
Mad at, mad about, mad with you.

A poem
A painting
A letter or two
To tell all I'm still with you
We are here
A mountain view
A dog barks
The rain
Starts and stops
Food cooks
In the house
What's my wish?

I am still with you.

DMZ Office

Office workers
Free fire zone
Our desks
Full of shrapnel holes
Bulls eye for an office decor
Thinks North Vietnamese artillery
Guns out
Fire away
10 minutes
Something different
The 122 rockets
The outhouse
Run for cover
Just office workers
Close to the DMZ.

Empty Streets

I walk in the early morning light the empty streets of
Saddlebrooke
For this the wish of thinking exercise, exercise, exercise
I walk in the company of one of my walking sticks
One thick and solid
Cut from fine black cherry resounds with a heavy thud
Proof it will be ready to crush you and him
And all the dangers of the shadows
What joy, the joy of the heavy stick.

For the fancy state of view
I carry a crooked stick
The projection of an artful bearing
Cut from Wisconsin currant
Rather unique
All very light
Passes with a tap, tap, tap
Softly it is gone, nice and quiet.

With the wood of Wisconsin
I walk the early morning of Saddlebrooke
Thankful for the support
When the wicked sun sneaks a peek over the mountains
Showing what the darkness hid
I return to the question of morning coffee
As I walk away
Tap, tap, tap
Beware! I carry a walking stick.

End of the Driveway

Wait on the edge of my world
For a message from beyond
One never knows if the wait will prove worth time invested.

Have already used more time than I have left
Use the remaining time well
Before it is gone.

When one is out of time any message from beyond usually has no value
My wait worthwhile for I'm engaged in the art of thinking,
Am I not?

I sit at the edge of my world, am I not interacting with it?
Started to rain,
That changes the progress and possibilities of the day.

The flashing light the message carrier is getting closer
I hope it gives me something to think about
And enlightenment for my thoughts.

But not today the other world beyond only wants my money.
So progress will have to come on a different path
With no help from the beyond.

Fresh from Sleep

Fresh from sleep
My wife becomes Cleopatra
Entering the room on a path of rose petals
Laid down with a husband's love.

He greets the morning
He stands close
Introducing the sun
When the shutters swing open.

To guide her day
He whispers his feeling
In a newly formed poem
Making her the center
Of all that will take place.

From Vietnam I Made It Back

It is best sometimes to look at what one has
Not what is missing
I am very rich in the important pieces of a good life
A VA hospital waiting room
A man my age also with PTSD
Also with Parkinson's, poor us?
No, fortunate me!
I have legs, a wife, a home
He had none.

Keeping in mind what I have
Please let me complain of a rough trip back to the States.

So in my stories of long ago
Is it too much that I write of a rough trip home
Maybe so
I wonder how his trip home went.

Hi-Diddle-Dee

Hi-diddle-dee
The icy wind blows for me
It bites my nose
Numbs the cheeks
Oh how grand
It thinks of me.

Winter cold has come today
We hope it does not stay
No time to play
Must work just to keep the cold away.

Think twice before a walk
Dress in layers deep
If warmth you want to keep.

The sun does shine without its heat
The world is cold
It is not a treat
Zero degrees for a high is no high at all
Until you see the low.

When walking on ice
Go very slow
To slip in the cold a big mistake.

Now stay away frost
I have to go into the house
Quick and close the door.

No it's not a trick you cannot see
With glasses frosted white
Just winter's way of saying deal with me

I Heard the Cry

I heard the cry
"I need your help"
Don't get many requests for help anymore
So this was important to me
A moving shape that carried the voice was leaving the side of the car
I struggled to get out to follow
With effort I made the side of the car
Only to find what was important to me
No longer there.

To my left across the street
A moving form called "I need your help with the door."
To reach the cry I needed to cross the street
The traffic was brisk
The drivers fast
After a few mis-starts I made it across to the corner
Of the large state office building "GEF1"
The sign did proclaim
I needed to turn the corner to provide help at the door
I made the steps
I turned the corner
Doors! Doors! Many doors high and low
Glass and steel
Which to take for my friend in need was not in view
With no direction to receive
No direction known
I must pick a door
I must pick a door to be of help
I must pick a door.

I Live in the Sky

I live in the sky
High
High above the clouds
High above the crowds
The pain
The needs
In the sky I fly
Above the mountain peaks
On the breeze
With the hawk.

Then one day
Soar with me
You and I
With the wind high
High in the sky
You and I
The wind.

I Move Very Little

I move very little
Slow when I do
I think a lot
Watching what goes around me.

How would it feel to walk forth
Standing without pain
Interact with the world around me
Using my movement in a free and fluid manner
I watch and let my imagination move me through the world
It all becomes what I want it to be
How long will existence be for me?
And time passes on and on.

Yes, this is the twilight of my time
True needs may be found and found to be small
For I know the end
If one is to know at all
I have my thoughts
These dreams of enchanted worlds that happen
When I can hold a pen
And still time passes on and on.

Slowly steadily the Parkinson's progresses
Maybe it would be better to talk not at all
And write only for myself in the silence of the night
I find peace and comfort in my thinking
When others discover depression in the twilight worlds I bring forth.

My breath short and speech not clear and strong
But for my mind and pen I go on
Time marches on.

I Saw Loneliness

Yesterday I saw loneliness
Felt the loss on one torn from his place in society
Pushed to the edge
Can you picture loneliness?

In a VA hospital
Loneliness like a thick vapor hung over the young veteran
What noble cause brought him to this?

I suspect reasons that make no sense
Nor does this picture

Young man in a wheelchair
Youth still touching the face
An old man behind his eyes

Sitting in a long hospital hallway
Next to a North facing window
Alone, wrapped carefully in a blanket
The building carries a chill this wet, wintry day

I see tubes going here and there
One draining urine
Is another for breathing?

Hours pass and I walk by again

Nothing moved or touched
Still facing North

In my battalion the saying goes
"If death was going to come, it would come from the North."

He looks
But not beyond the glass
Eyes open

People moving past
Even in a crowd
A picture of isolation, of loneliness

Here a flower stopped in mid blossom
By a cold hand
Still alive but never to bloom

I Took the Organic Waste

I took the organic waste to a far away place
To give it a home
A place to rest and rot
Where no man knows but the animals of the fields and brush
The bucket heavy and full
My back bent, my stride slow
The wind blew strong making the trip seem long
A chill in the air
Cold that was clear
The bucket I carried to the place the volunteer apples grow
Something only I know
But this is the end
No more will be dumped
I am leaving the land
Moving away to a place where people are many
Where things are done different with machines in the sinks
To grind the waste and one never leaves the house
With a bucket too heavy
They say this is so in many a town and city
But I will be 60 and have never done so
With a machine in the sink.

I have to say this doesn't sound natural like
My far away place for organic waste.

Ice Mountains

The ghost of ice mountains
A thousand years gone
Then heavy upon the land
The pressure
The pressure
Heavy!
Felt by rock and stone
Like a dark thought
Whose grip still holds memories
Influenced and shaped the world then and today
The ice mountain's work will not be changed soon or quick
Ghosts of the land that still touch the land
Even today we walk this earth touching the memories.

Lady from Catalina

A special Lady from Catalina walks the desert highways
With the need to travel
When the sun is high with a black and white parasol she walks
A flowing skirt and parasol
All finely done
She draws attention for her bearing and grace
Set in a curious location HWY 77 at a curious time of day
Temperatures 100 plus and the road surface more.

To ask her why is not my place
Why walk so regally with such poise in the heat of the day.
A special Lady from Catalina
Doesn't need a destination
Or so it seems
Does she have a starting point?
I begin to wonder
I could believe she just appears
Then is gone.

As the coyote one sees for a second
Running off the road
Now out of sight
Not needing a destination
But sharing the crooked smile of the Lady from Catalina.

Let Me Paint a Picture

Let me paint you a picture on nights without clouds
A dark sky for all to see
All who take the time or have the gift of time to spare
Look up!
The canvas opens
See planets, stars, the moon
All in their places
All in the order of here and now
Marching from east to west

Jupiter,
Saturn in company of Taurus with its red bull's eye Aldebaran
Off to the side one can spy
Bright clean light coming forth from star cluster, Pleiades

All on an endless chase
To follow Venus and the waxing moon through the night
Time marked and measured by the movement in the sky
If one wants to see time
This is how it is done on those clear nights
Time and much more is ours to view
For I have all the colors except for you.

Like a Peach

Words like a bite from a peach
Sweet, but messy
My body on the path
But easy to step over
Landscape of many observations
Some imagination, some the puck of dreams
Now victim of my literary schemes
Seed from the grandfather of ancient trees
Brought the rose-breasted grosbeak from the barn
Spirit guide to far and near
This catalyst of vision brings change
I face a door, open door
Wide stone stairs not up or down
Or here or there
Direction not clear
I find virtue in waiting
Bringing my train of thought to silence
A small voice reaches my ear
Travel one step into trust
It took me far, one step
It was like waking up
Thinking I could see 600 miles
I looked into a closet
Queer eyes looking out
Hearing laughter it made me smile
A distant call and the journey ends or does it now begin?
I first feel, then see the rose-breasted grosbeak at your feet
It casts a crimson glow
You look at me
Tension cuts the air
Our tomorrows pale before us
Then from me your gift, my forbearance
My good fortune, your smile
Breath comes again

To reach destiny
The world becomes our peach
Sweet, but messy

Like Air

Invisible things
Father's love
Like air
From the lungs
Gone in a breath
Was it ever there?
Final reflection
Not there
Life goes on
And you never see the air
That fills the lungs
Nor despair over love not there.

Long Walk

It's a long walk to a lonely street
When going nowhere it makes me think
Where have I been?

Not knowing what keeps me going
I stop when I should not
My friends not talking.

Directions unknown
Location not here or there
Dreams are happening out of sleep
Hard to know what to keep.

Not sure of place or spot
But need to arrive so I can stop
What direction to take is open to debate.

When all ends
To start again
Change I will
All I must from breath to view.

To find the path that brings me home
For in the end
It's a long walk to a lonely street.

Muse

Dear wife, true love of mine
I paint for thee and also for me
No others follow the brushes' stroke
To the ends you achieve in me

The color is nice and speaks to many
But it is the path of my brush
That wins your high praise
To what I owe these results I do not know
Only if there – be only one may that one be you.

My November

A cold, crisp mid-November morning
Sun still low in the eastern sky greets a cloudless day
Trees, grass, all the land coated white with a heavy frost
Most of the leaves have fallen from the trees
Only some oak still hold on
Grass brown
Toward the west
The gray brown tree line
Just now catching the first light of day
I see in great detail
Using my tripod mounted binoculars
Scanning slowly
When unexpectedly a splash of color dominates the view
The clear bright red of a cardinal
Gives excitement and focus to the earth tones
That fills my visual canvas before me
Then as if knowing it was being watched
The cardinal takes flight
But my loss is only for a moment
For into the room moves my own red cardinal
Ponderously moving across the room
Truly a cardinal that will never fly
My wife joins me dressed in her red robe
Providing the color for my day
And contrast to the earth tones of my November.

Near Me?

The day my voice is stilled and breath no longer drawn
The day my thoughts happen no more
Will you still think of me?
Knowing my thoughts once had voice and form
Can we comfort each other after the end?
Feeling a breeze
The warmth of day
My closeness in your thoughts on moments we shared
When all that is now is no more
When all the trees we planted grow old and die
Even then will you still be near me?
In what way I cannot say
Will we know each other?
Find each other?
Share comfort after the end or will death be the end?
Complete nonexistence?
If so it gives me no comfort to think it now without you.

Oh Spare Me

"Oh spare me," whines the pampered sophisticate
"I have heard it all before" she intones the refrain
A jaded view of life demands new and clever topics
To make life worth her time.

No cliches in her lexicon
Only in her computer's "tell me how to write" program
Which is followed much like a robot follows a data stream
How sad! What little imagination
To reach this state of boredom
Do they reach boredom?
Or are they themselves boredom
And pleasant words only turn to such
When arriving at their highbrow gate
But as I have said before
Viewed from afar it is hard to tell the intent of a circus.

Old Warriors Fade Away

A VA Hospital waiting room
A stiff quiet man wore
A cap letters proclaiming "USMC"
He looked the right age
For my war
So I loosen my lips
And verbally jump in
The risky waters of conversation
"Been to Viet Nam?"
From there we do the
Check out comparing
Dates and names
Then we can talk
Talked about shared experiences
Feelings, nothing deep
That would be awkward
He said something about Agent Orange
But it was easy to see the
Mist between the eyes and
The mind
His mind was somewhere else
The surgery this afternoon
They called his name
He moved slow but straight
Thru the doors of ambulatory surgery

Time passed in uneven progression
Slow in the waiting room
Fast in surgery
To the Marine's wife a nurse
Came out and handed over a ring
Saying he wants you to have this

Such impressions set the tone
My thoughts bouncing around
Memories of an old war
To this afternoon and why I was
Here in ambulatory surgery
None of this gave much comfort
For here old warriors come for health and care
These walls witness to lives failing
And breaking
I watch men around me
Being told to expect less
All at some level
It seems to feel
It was not supposed to be like this
Now we were no longer
On a first name basis
With comfort and joy
Many have watched their
Last days slip away

The smell of urine fills the halls
With tubes poking and prodding
Not a place visited by comfort
The world is just beyond these walls
Life goes on
Don't expect special tenderness
The world outside is busy doing
The things busy people do
Think we become invisible

No special awareness
The world turns and moves
With a purpose for today
And tomorrows
We cannot ask different

That would go against
The nature of the race

The human race
So old, men warriors of
Yesteryear stay behind
The walls and fade
Fade away

On the Road

On the road
Eyes wide open
So is the mind
Seeking knowledge when the room is still
And the small voices can be heard
Talking to high and low

Think of must be questions
Searching answers on this busy dance hall floor

But the days come and go
Then down a lonely road to nowhere
At a rest stop not there
An old man hard used by his travels
Old man there, then not
Called me close until I felt the silence
Of the juke box stopped
While waiting for a nickel to be found

He whispered in my ear
Told me of my days and their numbers
Some answers may be best not known
Some knowledge can wear a person down
It hit me hard
Much like freezing rain
On a paper thin jacket
All changed and turned
My direction lost
Values unknown
The questions I didn't ask
The meaning of answers
Who has the map?

For the end is sooner and as unexpected
As the thread bare blanket

Found one day unable to hold warmth
It is tossed aside
For the rich or the poor
For the loved or the lonely
It comes much the same
It's the rag heap and out the door.

But existence being a fickle maid to fate
Leaves the meaning of the end up to us.

Order

Give me order
We are back to normal
I want to be awake
To drink my morning coffee
Faye rushed off to work
My coffee cooled into an afterthought of the day.

Out of Shadows into the Light

Husband gone many years
Old crone wise and gray
Back now bent, the burden of long life hard work
Slowly walks the long farm road alone
Missing the company she shared
When they walked this path together
A thousand times before
Road now pressed in from both sides
By branch and limb from tree and brush
It is the walk from the house he built
For his young wife
To the edge of their land
The edge of their world
Now a world she rarely leaves
But for that most rural function
The mail box the sole connection to the world outside
But today she feels something

Feelings like a soft glove from
The past brush at the memory
Is he close, waiting?
The barn to the left
She leaves the shadows to enter the sunlight
Not just the light offered by the east field
But by the passing of years
Now she walks to the light
A thick fog of moving dancing light
Carrying no fear she feels the comfort
The safety he always extended to her
There he is her soul mate
They reach out touching
Together again
After all those dark nights alone
They walk the path side by side
As they did a thousand times before
On the farm overgrown
At the edge of the world.

Parkinson's Disease Gives
– version 2

It gives the gift of humility
It demands of the proud to look again at our existence
Rediscover what is important

Parkinson's disease also has us look again at comfort
It takes away the comfort of the body
Puts it out of reach never to be fully found again
Yet it gives time as a backhanded gift
Time to find comfort in spirit, if not the body

Parkinson's disease lets us know
That every day we can still care for ourselves is a gift
A gift that may not be given tomorrow
For tomorrow we may not be able to do the simplest tasks
Tasks done so proudly just yesterday
Gone like a dream upon awakening

Parkinson's disease also helps us see
The worth of true friends and companions
Who are there not because of your polished speech
Or beautiful and able body
But what they can see in our inner person
Let's hope we have the wisdom
To appreciate our friends and companions

We are people that once had control
Over our daily habits and broader aspects of our day
That had a place in running the world
In large or small ways
Now with Parkinson's disease
It is a new experience
A big adjustment

Remember the gift of humility
Learn to value and enjoy each day
One day at a time

The Plow Turns Time

The first day of Spring 2004
A windy day
My thoughts focus on the soil of the fields
The west field for sure.

Frost still in the ground
I wait for the time
When the soil slides across the face of the plow
And the robin stands ready to feed on the worm
Telling all the frost is out.

Start plowing now
Sink the plow deep and turn the farrow complete
So what lay beneath
Now lies on top.

It's like turning back time
What lies in the soil
Will make this Spring complete
Bringing a crop of worked stone
The tools of yesterday.

Pushy Poet

In a fast paced world
No time to slow
To think or stop
Pushy a poet has to be
To trick and capture
Just to place his poems in special spots
That his words may ensnare the people on the run
And spill some thought and prose in their way
Upon their day
Though it may be self-serving
It's good for them
It's good for us
That we push the labor of rhyme
As hard as the world pushes us
And never say you're sorry
To cause the world to reflect
Please forget about respect
Or money in accounts
Ours is a true calling
If such can be said
Before we are dead.

Rapping

In my bedroom with the TV on
I nod in and out of sleep, comfort sits with me in my lazy-boy
recliner
Then awake with a start!
Who is rapping, rapping on the outside wall?
But then I know from past events
It is that rowdy group of flicker woodpeckers.
Banging on the cedar siding
I could scream, I could yell, but it would be to no avail
The brazen birds have learned to ignore me
It's sad to say
Upon learning the identity of the culprits
Faye issues the refrain "darn birds"
Myself, I'm just happy they don't drill holes in the siding
So for small gratitudes and rude awakenings, the story ends
Lazy-boy and I find comfort
And finish our nap.

Saddlebrooke Dog

Saddlebrooke dog
Much attention to you
Could you have it any better?
Lying in the sun
Old bones say no
But deep in your collective canine memory
Feel the pull of old instincts
Feelings that have no place in your Saddlebrooke days
The urge to run
Run free
No leash
Run in any direction
To seek whatever you pleased
Whenever you wanted
You smell me
You know I lived
I deeply know places in your memory
I could tell where the rabbit hides
Where cool fresh water flows
Where the deer lay to rest
And why the owl calls and where she nests.

But today I sit at the table
Talking of literary things
You watch from the rug
Peace we find in our Saddlebrooke days
Yet we both know there is more.

So much attention
Saddlebrooke dog
Could it be any better?
Being in the sun
Old bones say no
But deep in collective canine memory

Feels the pull
Of old instincts
Feelings with no place
In Saddlebrooke days
Urge to run, run free
No leash, any direction
To seek what you please.

Scythe for Death

Mr. Death looks so fine, I know; I see him, not blind for with my droopy little eye I do spy. Mr. Death outside my kitchen window watching, watching doing nothing but watching. As stiff as steel one could say as he tries to hide in the day lilies. In his silent nonverbal way he speaks of joy he speaks of fun he speaks to me. Who said death doesn't take a holiday? Death needs a place but not this place. I may ask him to move very soon one of these days; yes that's right face death, send him packing and I'm not just talking. Outside my kitchen window is no place to take a holiday; and the birds show no respect.

Shower House in Vietnam

In Rain
Walk
In cold wind
Walk
Stand naked
Under cold water
Stand naked
In wind
Do it again
Another day
Ask why
Ask why
Do it again
Never again
Time gone
Place gone
Lose memory
All gone.

Something Simple

Something simple in the country
A slower pace no need to race
Tend the wood stove
Quietly done
Wood stored and easy to reach
No need to rush
Fruits of summer ready for eating
Put up when days were long
The cherries pitted, peaches peeled and quartered
Apples pressed for cider or cut thin for drying
Grapes and pears were used fresh
Whatever the method
Fruit ready for winter days
Our firewood close at hand
The mid December nights are growing long
A dog barks across the creek
The farm next door
I don't listen for my dog to reply
She barks no more
The loss makes us sad
Who will guard the garden?
Who will chase the deer at command?
The job is left undone
The deer know
Four in the garden yesterday
They had the look of comfort and ownership
The old cat is still around
Soon he will be at the window making his demands
Feed me now
Feed me now
Simple day
Simple needs
Peace and change in the country.

Sour Grapes and Belly Aches

The words break free in poetry and
Speak for me
They reflect in some way who I am, what I value
Style has to be easy, comfortable, a joy to write
Just has to please me.

My words don't tend toward the complex
Simple words suit me
In style and format that's right for me.

I am not, nor ever will be, I believe
A kindred spirit of critics so lettered and endowed with published work
Nor a comfortable selection for a judging jury
They could not identify with me.

So protest I do with simple words
With no phrases or clever turns
To tell of troubled minds in twisted relationships
It's plain, with different words I do pursue.

Also the prose that seems to be in vogue
Comes from tongues so trained, so clever
That the simple undirected reader
Knows not what he reads.

If this is so it also seems these poets of the day
Are bound together in common points of view
Is this a hoax on the many
The hijacking of an art form
Are they interesting only to themselves
Viewed from afar it's hard to tell the intent of a circus
This s a circus of many fools
Or are they truly deep thinkers?

So who is circus clown?
Answer as you will
I will write what pleases me and hope it troubles you.

Prince of Poppycock

I am prince of poppycock
I am very full of it
I fall on my merits
Or stop the decline by sitting on my
Behind
Then with my head in the clouds
I am full of ups and downs
Some look forward to slowing me down
What they don't know
It is not my body going up and down
It is my mind, my imagination
That rubs them so raw
I will only change, if at all,
When that tight-rope walking mob
Falls headfirst into my
Trash bin of incomplete nonsense
These people claim and shout
I waste time I make no sense
True sometimes to some minds
But until there is something better to do
I will keep salting your wounds of intolerance
And poke your pompous outrage
As some say mine is an art
It comes naturally

I Give You Planets

The planets on a string
Lined up in the night sky
Pretty rocks with holes for a string
Answers and explanations with no strings
All things simple
Strings or not
I have trouble with the knots
When my task calls for a knot to bind
I call Faye to the task
The sum is greater than the parts
Believe it or not
Keep it simple
No strings attached
No tangles to unwrap
Simple and focused you and I

Wind and Snow
February 2003

Wind and snow
Faye walks
I watch from window
Warm wood fire close
Competing with the soft background music
House quiet inside
Faint howl of the wind outside
Cold outside
Faye well dressed
Walks stiffly against wind and snow
Her boots covered by the building drifts
She moves carefully
One sure step after the other
Progress slow
1200 feet to travel in whiteout
Sun set half an hour ago
Darkness deepening
I see her clear for a moment
Then gone
Engulfed in swirling snow
A winter walk home
After a long day at work and return on winter roads
I feel like running out to help
Not prepared
Not a good idea
Now time has its reward
She makes it to the door
Glasses fogged over
But a smile at our greetings
Close the door to the storm
Settle in for the night
Winter in Wisconsin

I Did Spy

I did spy with my very fine eye
A droopy faced man with a droopy little eye

With voice of strength and youth I did think,
"Your arm, what is wrong, are you hurt?"

With a soft low response the crooked old man did reply,
"It is stiff, only stiff and weak."

Strange his voice sounded so close,
"Don't lose your balance. Maybe you should sit?
Where do you go so slow, crooked old man?"

His weak reply:
"I have nothing to gain staying. I go on.
Who stands before you is a stranger to myself."

His reflection broken
He left the edge of the water,
The same time I did.

Sharp

Sharp
Ill defined
Dangerous to deal with
Long lasting

Damage is still happening
Dealing with emotional shrapnel
Like the jagged steel pieces from Vietnam
To battlefields of life

Emotional shrapnel was hot
When it burned its way in
Hard to remove
Jagged edges embedded themselves into existence
On impact
Turned off feelings

Now a price is paid every day
Until the demons are confronted
Or death takes all away

Starting

The gray fog of predawn slowly absorbing the blackness of night turning the eastern sky into a temporary twilight, which is soon lost to the bright sunlight of dawn, the signal post of a new day. A rare gift from earth and sun to be used well. Remembered as special, for it may never happen again.

Streets with No People

The streets with no people
An hour before sunset
The sky clear
The light breeze a comfort
I sit on the porch watching the quiet streets
House after house
No people, no cars, no noise
Used but unused places
The best money can buy, but empty
Where are the people?
Do they have so much that it can't all be used?
The streets empty
Then movement on the wide road
A coyote comes walking down the broad pavement
Not used, not now by people or cars
Coyote uses the paved path to good ends
It seems so sure of itself that all roads made for coyote
Which along with the rabbit and quail
Find the well-landscaped lots suited to their needs
With little interference from the HOA.

Sunlight

Sunlight streaks in and out
So it seems a fast moving game
The storm clouds in a cold winter sky

The effect on the ground
Moving patterns
Sometimes light sometimes shade
A patch work always changing
Very complex
Teases the eyes
Challenges the mind

Then increasing the visual performance
Wind blowing strong
Now no wind at all
Big gusts! Then calm
Trees and plants dance to the force not seen
A dancing shadow appears with the sun out
Shadow gone just as quick as clouds move in.

A visual display of great energy
Changing how we see the everyday
Nature appears in transformation by the rule of sun, wind and sky
To our imagination the land becomes the canvas
Touched by many strokes, colors and brushes
All painting a picture of nature
Nature seeking balance does inspire
Symmetry does not rule this day
On a windy day
Chaos rules are in effect
Freedom guides the brush stroke when chaos rules

The Bright Sun

The bright Wisconsin sun never warms the cold crisp air
Land covered and quiet under a deep blanket of snow.

Tucson dry land
Prickly plants, cactus plants
Watch your step
Things that bite and sting
Temperatures run from hot to hotter
Find the shade quick
Stay out of the sun
When the rocks are too hot to handle.

I recall Wisconsin when winter cold would come
When the icy wind blows it bites the nose
Numbs the cheeks
Zero degrees for a high – is no high at all
Until you feel the low.

Arizona summer
Walk, visit, shop before 10 a.m.
Don't fight the heat
Stay off the streets
Arizona is where you want to be if you want to be close to the sun
Or seems to be
With rocks too hot to handle.

Yes I recall days gone by
Years gone by
In Arizona much is different
Not sure of my tomorrows
The ambiguity I measure with comparisons
The cold the past
The heat my tomorrows.
But where do I lead you?

I lead you nowhere but to remember
Times are good if you still care
That the rocks are too hot to handle.

The Cowboy

With a smile on his face
The cowboy pushes the grocery cart across the hot asphalt parking lot
Cars criss-crossing here and there
His name it came to be found is Walter from Tucson
He has a knowing look for the basic, but important things in life
He gave off the sense he could see the good side of hard times
And have a joke to spare.

It was plain to see he was no stranger to hard work
But also knew its rewards
For a new pickup truck carries a price tag and his was very new
Before he caught my eye
His bearing and presence caught Faye's attention in the store
Through effort and plan she stood behind him in the check out line
Where he seemed well known and well liked
Faye and Walter exchanged smiles
She also picked up a sense of a working man with quiet merit
A man one would want to call friend.

The Moon Is High

The moon is high in the sky
The mink close to the ground hunts all around
Bear smells in the woods searching
Mink don't do your business there
Ugly bear can crush outlook and hope
So rush your business done
Then come have some fun
Clear the area until the bear is gone
But then a mink belongs in the woods
What to do what to do.

Ask Venus in the east
The mink is in sight of Venus tonight
As it happens this very warm day
Explaining with a tail such detail that it follows forms
Many an opinion in the woods under the moonlight follow a
detail form
Ideas are closed on Sunday
Today only Monday
Push tail out of sight
Bear smells now he comes
Run push and shove clawing soft marks upon the moon
Mink and bear mix as one
So remember mink could dance all night in time
What is a mink but time
Fun and a quick bit of feelings
Bears can't dance under the moon or drink from broken cups
The broken cups of our imagination
So let the mink and bear fill your imagination with these lines.

Time Hard Partner

Time, hard partner to share existence
Solid bodies need steady place in the fabric of being
Partnership with time can't be avoided
Circle of life
Nothing ends as nothing
Man knows the end
No escape
One way out
Many retreat to grand delusions
Religious dogmas
What answer is god's answer?
Doesn't answer questions
Look the other direction
See puzzle of life
Accept the terms
Be the answer
Lose your secrets
Fit with nature
Sever the dish with no limits
Time runs out
Now, now, now.

Truth

The person that holds no absolute
Truths is truly free to seek truth
This person can ask all things, all questions
Thus the person that cannot ask

All questions are not completely open to truth
That is there is a "truth"

What irony
All of this fades with my coffee.

Two Who Watched

When fear has not yet found you
Yet seems to hound you
With hell on earth calling
Seek escape if not for the body
For the mind
Here unfolds a story

In a land I call yesterday
Vietnam a war of death and waste
Took many to a strange place
All of us in and under a tin roof hut
Fourteen souls seek sanctuary for body and spirit
In many ways
Little found and little comfort
NVA Artillery shelling wore us down
We find stress a wicked toll taker
Now at evenings' rest
A little magic spills our way
If magic the word we be the takers
Six men went high
Six went low
And two of us watched

Smoking weed the six went high
Like clouds of sweet smoke
They got very high
In the mind's eye they reached marmalade skies
Saw colors of sunsets
Received peace and sleep
And two of us watched.

Six got so low
Had to look up to see the tops of empty beer cans piled high
As they sank in the mud

The mud and beer covered their thoughts
Took away feelings
Until they didn't know
Nor did they care
And the two of us watched

The two who watched
Were Taylor and Woods
And Taylor wasn't always there
At times he left the light on
But he was gone to who knows where
When Taylor was gone
Was Woods still there?
And no one watched

Luck be with us
The wolf did not walk that night.

Waiting Room

In the waiting room
The crackle of crone blasts through the other sounds
Then in competition
A want to be rapper who washes windows
VA hospital windows
Begs for attention with his on and off noise

It seems we brought everything from home
Sitting together
Thoughts much the same
Intent to contain things and stuff inside my cloth bag
Trying the limits I said enough
Enough for the cloth bag

Keeping calm, keeping cool
Sitting or standing, waiting
Slowly the hours pass
Yet life goes on so fast

Think of home
Place of rest and dreams
Between here and there
Traffic jams the I-10
So learn to enjoy here
Until we get there
Faye sits, book in her lap
Thoughts across the room
A penny for her thoughts
She shares
A sign reads "health E-vet" a computer thing
But it also reads "heal the vet"

Now I notice other noise
Cell phones how rude!

So is the price of free health care
Or did I pay?
Another time, another place.

We Move Again?

If we move again
We move as one
If not together
I would stop
No moving.

Stress is heavy
The tasks are many.

Movers came today
You were sweet
I started strong
At the end went to sleep
You carried the day
I faded away.

Think of our gain
Beautiful house I have to say
Thousand more square feet.
In the end I find myself thinking
What cupboard has the plates?

What Irony

What irony
The shaky hand man pours the big girl's coffee
She chooses what cup to use
Because she's a big girl
Not a cracked cup
Not a special cup
Not a big cup, but big enough.

Minutes pass
Coffee cools into an afterthought for the day
She found a cup
Big girl gets her way
She remembers shaky hand man
Drinks the warm coffee
In the cup of her choosing
Her way, her day.

Windows on the Plane

The windows on the plane are thick but so are the clouds
Then they are not what you think you see
May not be what to think
The big can look small
And the small you cannot see at all
Know where you are high or low, north or south
Think deep to find the center of that thunderhead or the distant
Mountain peaks
May the thinking tell, where you fit in the big and small of it all
Looking down from 7 miles up.

Years Become Many

When the years become many
And the body is bent
The portent of a new day
Is greeted with a silent "thank you"
When the stars in the east sky
Start to fade I am greeted by the knowledge
I made it through the night
It was another night
That heaven and earth allowed me
To share the bed with you
For age and health take their toll
One night will be the last I share with you
How sad that I know this.

Stories

Coyotes

THIS IS ANOTHER STORY about those two goodlooking young men, Norbert Lopez and me. It must have been about 1962 and again we were in the Tortolita Mountains, our private hunting domain or that is how we thought about it. What promoted that view was that we never saw another person during all the time we spent in those mountains. Norbert's father worked for the Nelson Ranch, and at that time outsiders were not allowed to cross ranch land to get to the Tortolitas.

An unusual event took place that I can't explain. For some reason, we were not following two of our unwritten rules. First, I was walking in the mountains by myself, and second, I was without my gun. All I can recall under these rule-breaking conditions was that my trip would take me to some location in the mountains, after which I would go back and rejoin Norbert.

It was a nice day for a walk. It was a cooler time of year and I was traveling a major trail almost wide enough for a four-wheel drive vehicle, even though it wasn't generally used by people or vehicles. Norbert was a mile back up this path, and there was no one but me for ten miles. This was before cell phones, GPS, and all that kind of stuff. What I did have was a bottle of water and a strong young body that could walk or run miles in this Sonoran desert mountain terrain.

A mile from my starting point, I noticed a coyote off the path on my right. I had the feeling he had been watching me for some time already. As I kept walking, it almost seemed as if he had been waiting for me. When I made it far enough down the trail, he started walking down the slope toward the path. He came toward me in a slow, non-threatening manner. There seemed to be intelligence behind his eyes and purpose in his actions. I began to feel this had all been planned. He was studying me also. After his study, he seemed to know more about me than I did of him. He had very interesting eyes and expressions.

Something out of the ordinary was taking place. When he was forty feet away, he came no closer, but matched my speed in moving on the path.

I felt this very unusual coyote was my escort as we walked side by side, forty feet apart, down the trail, still in the mountains and going down a slope slowly out of a valley that was getting wider. In a short time the right side of the path rose up thirty feet and became a low hillside. Over that hillside was the greatest assemblage of coyotes I had ever seen or heard about. They were all watching me with varying expressions and showed great interest in my arrival. In numbers, there had to be forty to sixty coyotes. Each coyote had its own space on that hillside, a place to sit and overlook everything below them. Because of that they were spread over the entire hillside, top to bottom, end to end. It was a very impressive sight. Maybe I am wrong, but what I know of coyotes, not only was the number of coyotes rare but the fact that it was around noontime and they were out and active was very unusual.

On one level I knew that, if I triggered the wrong reaction in them, they could tear me apart. I kept walking and maintained only indirect eye contact, but showed no fear. That hand played and I got out of danger.

Another observation: they knew right away that I had no weapon. I've encountered a lot of coyotes in the mountains, and they were always cautious when I was carrying a gun.

On another level the entire event was so unusual it seemed to be metaphysical. I may not have evidence, but from what I saw and felt the following listed points may be true. The entire event was planned and set up for it to happen as it did. There was a greater intelligence to those coyotes than would be normal.

This question remains with me: Was there some purpose or meaning in my coming across all those coyotes?

Now, forty years later, I have another coyote story, this on our farm in Wisconsin.

To get the morning paper, Cinder, my dog, and I left the house quietly, not wanting to wake our house guests, the McDowells. Cinder was subdued, walking on only three legs, the left rear not working, much as my left side. Starting down the drive in the early morning sunlight, we looked down from the hilltop to the newly planted fields, which showed last year's corn trash mixed into the wet brown soil. I could hear the resident geese, honking as they walked the fields looking for last year's corn. Then something new caught my eye, a light brown shape twice the size of Cinder. It turned and looked at me. I had come across a beautiful coyote this quiet morning.

The coyote looked back at the geese, and then with great quickness it ran at the geese. I never saw an animal run so fast. It was a smooth run over the soft field, very fast, the geese barely got in the air before the speeding coyote was under them. Then he came to a surprisingly quick stop under a goose that was trying to gain some height from the ground. The coyote stopped and jumped all in a flash. He must have jumped twelve feet straight up and just missed the goose. The speedster didn't think twice about the lost food and with no hesitation kept on moving west at breakneck speed. Upon reaching the brush of the wetland, it quickly disappeared.

I was amazed at the speed and smoothness of the coyote's run. The morning excitement over, I thought myself lucky. Cinder at my side, I started walking on to see what else I could see when no one else was out walking but me.

Art

||||||||||||||||||||||||||||||||||||||||||||||||||||||||||||||||||||||||||||||||||||||||||||||||||||||||||||||||||||||||||||||||||||||

YEARS AGO, I WAS LUCKY. I would get to work with my Grandpa Art making hay. I was happy to help and spend time with him, maybe get to know him better.

I was about fourteen years old and spent hours helping, also riding the ponies or just exploring my grandparents' small farm, which was just outside Amherst, Ohio. The summer there can be hot and very humid. My grandfather, Arthur Roth, was – from my point of view – intelligent, modest, but with a sense of humor. We were not close, but he always treated me well. I thought, Here is a man who uses his head to earn a living – a white collar worker. I had seen the insides of factories and knew the conditions for blue collar workers were not good. Grandpa Art's job had something to do with the docking and unloading of the large iron ore boats at the steel mill in Lorain. He went to work every day, decade after decade. At the end of the work day, he would work on the farm. It was a very low tech farm. I don't remember one power tool or tractor. He was a reliable, hardworking man who loved his wife. I believe parts of my life have been copied from his values and his example, if not directly from him, then through my mother.

Making hay by hand is very hard work. My grandpa, while not physically inspiring, was a steady uncomplaining worker. I spent long tiring hours in the field trying to keep up. He was 56 years older than I was, and though. I thought of myself as strong and full of energy, it was all I could do to finish the job with him. My body silently protested those times when I had to go back in the field to start another step in getting the entire job done – the hay cut, dried, raked, and loaded in the loft of the barn. How youth can misjudge the elderly. During all this work together, I don't recall anything he said to me, not one word, but I do remember his example.

Twenty years later I know that I, too, was a white collar worker. I owned a farm and found myself making a lot of hay. It still was hot, dirty work, even with three tractors and all the power equipment. I may have followed your path, Grandpa Art, for twenty-five years, but now I watch others do the work. I spend time with my art, short stories, and poems. I like to think I took it to the next level, and he would have enjoyed it, too. Why else did we call him "Art"?

Emergency Room

||||||||||||||||||||||||||||||||||||||||||||||||||||||||||||||||||||||||||||||||||||||||||||||||||||||||||||||||||||||||||||||||||||||

MAY 2007, JUST TWO YEARS of living at Saddlebrooke and we are already testing the EMT services here in Arizona.

Uncertainty filled my thinking. Something was wrong. My health was in steep decline. My wife, Faye, worried and wanted me to explain what was happening. I could not think and would not listen. Stress climbed and in my mind a silent scream rang out, "Doom! Doom!"

Drug interactions were causing blood pressure problems that might shut me down. When my blood pressure reached 55 over 27, I found peace. I lay down and did not worry, move, or talk. Peace was in a different world for my wife, and all the problems of this world were on her. With no help from me, she got the emergency people to our house. With great effort the EMT's flipped me from my bed onto the gurney. The ride out of the house was wild. Banging the front door, the gurney moved fast down the drive. Would this be my last ride?

I was being pulled back into a noisy uncomfortable world. Activity threatened my peace. It was all very unpleasant. They got me to the hospital emergency room so fast there was no wife to answer questions. She made a wrong turn leaving our house after the ambulance left and had to back track to find me. Normally, my job was telling her where to turn. Soon she was at the hospital and answering their questions. I was still quiet.

Emergency rooms are set up to save lives, but we felt ourselves falling deeper into the complicated web of medical care. For my wife and me, uncertainty was now the centerpiece of our day. Choices were few and not of our choosing. Would I walk the hallways of our home by the end of the day?

The slow movement of time started to tell in our favor. The chance of going home was looking good. Now three hours into my "no blood pressure" adventure, I was still on the hospital gurney hooked up to a monitoring machine.

It is hard enough for a person with Parkinson's disease to find comfort. I was approaching my limit; this uncomfortable condition was going to have negative effects on my health. Very tight and stiff muscles can cause many problems. I also tried to pass on information that Parkinson's can cause false readings on their machines. My wife and I were in a back room when she started to rub my left foot, trying to keep the muscles relaxed. Those gurneys are not the most comfortable, and I don't think emergency room people understand the stress stiff muscles bring. My arms were loaded with medical patches and needles, so I asked her to scratch my head. As she did, the alarms went off and people started rushing into the room. I told them I was okay. Not listening, they didn't hear me and pushed my wife away.

In the turmoil of the moment, I remember seeing someone who brought calmness. As my gurney moved within a few feet of a dark-haired woman lying still, her eyes opened, drinking in deeply the world around. She looked calm and wise. In that moment our eyes locked and our worlds passed. She watched as I was rushed by in a crowd of people. My crowd was raising a hue and cry, casting an aura of crisis while my chest lay bare to their concerns and efforts. My arms were full of needles, recording straps, and cuffs.

Uncertain as to the outcome or what would be imposed on me, I had to keep this well-intentioned mob from taking what was mine. Either my words got through to them or maybe the numbers did not support what they were doing. Somewhat confused and embarrassed, they melted away out of the room. No one said, "Hello" or "How are you? Wasn't that breathtaking?" No, they just ordered more tests, and I spent more time lying in a general state of discomfort.

Uncertainty is a fearful thing, especially giving control to the hospital staff, to people I did not know and had not built any trust in. I signed some paperwork. What was that all about? Afraid of this and burdened with confusion, my thinking was not the best. I turned to the one I could trust, wanting her to take charge of all that happened, to take away the monitors and needles of my day. I made these demands on poor Faye, who was just as much a victim of the day as I. We were prisoners bound by chains of uncertainty. Out of fear or ignorance, I made demands on her. She already had a crushing load to carry.

But in time luck broke our way, and we were able to escape the medical care system that kept me alive and sent me home again. Roughed up and worn out, we were able to walk through the door of our home one more time. It felt good.

Remember the dark-haired woman lying still in the emergency room? I saw her picture in the obituary column last month. She sounded like a very special person, whose passing is a loss to all of us.

Making Hay

||||||||||||||||||||||||||||||||||||||||||||||||||||||||||||||||||||||||||||||||||||||||||||||||||||||||||||||||||||

ON A HOT SUMMER DAY, the farm fields are quiet. The yellow grain heads of the oats move slowly with the breeze. The grasses of the hayfields stand tall and green, undisturbed.

The fields are a place of solitude. Every day I look upon these calm places, seeing change come, as it does, slowly with the seasons. These are my buffers to the fast-paced world beyond. The outside world does not look long or hard at a grass field. These fields provide space without drawing attention, but now they are being watched – the west, east, south, and north fields.

Then one day the weather is right, the condition of the fields ready, and man has entered the fields. He brings noise and big machines that have seen rough, hard work. He brings activity. The grass comes first. The mower, nine feet wide, cuts everything in its path, and every square foot, every inch is cut, one end to the other. Every plant falls to the ground. The field has changed in a day.

Next comes the oats; in lumbers the combine, a very tall large machine, moving slowly over the slopes and tight spots, cutting the oats and pulling them in. The oat grain stays in the combine while all the rest flies out the back onto the field. In a few hours all the oats are gone, loaded on a large tractor trailer truck parked by the barn.

Now all the plant life has been cut. The grass dries in the sun; the oat straw lies in the field waiting for the baler. The farmer hopes for good weather, for the rain to stay away as the sun dries the grass, turning it into hay. The cut fields have a day or two of quiet.

Then slowly, softly like the beginning of a new movement in a symphony, it begins again. A small tractor pulling a hay rake starts raking the straw and then the hay into long rows for the baler to pick up. The tractor and baler cross the fields, wrapping all into neat packages, round bales, square bales, or sometimes both. Agricultural production is a noisy time. Farm equipment and men cover the ground. Hot and covered with dust, they work long hours. When all is finished, the fields are quiet, changed. One wonders, will the grass grow back? Will the field recover from this assault?

The fields are stressed, they need rain, but another crop has been harvested, all except for one round bale of straw, a runaway. Five feet wide, six feet tall, and weighing maybe 800 pounds, it was easy to spot the hilltop field behind the house. I was watching from inside the house, since I could no longer physically help with the field work. But I could view the large bale of straw being wrapped with twine fifty feet from my window. As the round baler started opening its rear door to release the bale, I knew from past experience there might be problems. The tractor and baler were down slope when the large straw bale was released. The machinery moved away, leaving the round bale free to roll down the slope. Slowly, it began to move. I worried for the grapes, which were in its path, but it soon moved past them, gaining speed. Was it headed for the garden? It looked like it, but then it veered toward the garden shed.

Ron, the tractor driver, saw this happening. He increased the speed of the tractor and made a sharp right turn. He drove across the lawn, pulling in front of the fast-moving bale. The huge tractor was able to stop it cold, and the runaway bale fell on its side.

The bale, roughed up and partially unwrapped, was later carried away. It was taken to a staging area with all the other round bales of straw. The next day, all the bales except for the runaway bale were loaded on a trailer and taken away. Now the runaway sits at the edge of the field, a lonely sight. All through summer it sits, a reminder of the day it broke loose, moving through its own world, on its own path. That day the runaway bale had an adventure. Many of us can relate, knowing how one day of adventure can change what our tomorrows will be.

Trip Back to Ohio

WITH THE TELLING OF THIS STORY from the spring of 1963, I will tie my new life in Arizona to the fourteen years I lived in Amherst, Ohio. Mr. and Mrs. John Smythe, who at that time lived in Amherst but spent winters in Tucson, were getting ready to break camp in Tucson and fly back to Ohio. John, who was related to my mother, was also a well-known attorney and, at one time, a judge in Amherst. It was already April, and they still did not have anyone to drive their late model Oldsmobile back to Amherst. They were both in their seventies, I believe, and did not want to drive a 2000-mile trip to Ohio.

To my great surprise, they approached me through my mother and offered me the job of driving the car back to Ohio. My friend, Norbert Lopez, would go with me. We would be paid for our expenses, including bus tickets back to Tucson. Of course, we jumped at the opportunity. We took our task seriously and, with everyone's help, planned the trip.

This was forty-five years ago. I don't remember all the details, but that has never stopped me before. I have two stories to recount about this trip. The first I should call "Poor Judgment." The other would be "Helen Roth's Respect for Norbert."

"Poor Judgment" puts us halfway to Ohio. We were on a back road, some state highway in eastern Kansas. This road was more like a small country road in Wisconsin, running through farmland with trees and brush growing close to the road. As Norbert and I were passing through a small town, myself doing the driving, a carload of young men started driving close to us and calling out stupid phrases, much as young men do when meeting others in town. The boys in the local car made inquiries as to the size and speed of our car. I just wanted to get out of their neighborhood. Nevertheless, somehow I was pulled into racing them.

This is not typical for me. I never raced anyone before or after this incident. However, I wanted remove myself from this entanglement as soon as possible. We raced outside of town. The road, which I liked earlier because it was straight and any other traffic on the road was easily visible, now went downhill into a river-bottom valley. Here the other boys tried to pass us, giving it all they had.

The big Oldsmobile stayed six to ten feet in front of the other car. They could not pull close enough to try to pass. I look and saw we were going over 100 mph. Then the nature of the road changed quickly. The road was now ten feet higher than the surrounding land, with the land on both sides a flat flood plain, heavy with brush. I glanced to the right and saw the other car crashing through the brush. We were rapidly approaching the river. It was then that I noticed a small sign reading "one-lane bridge." The bridge was long, maybe 400 feet, and very narrow. There must have been other signs that probably said "cars only." The bridge had a lot of steel grid work closing in the roadway, both top and sides. The road surface looked and felt like railroad ties. The bridge was so narrow that, sitting dead center, the big Oldsmobile had only six inches clearance on either side. I had to put everything out of my mind and focus on threading the needle at 90 mph. Norbert was smart in that he did not distract me, however I heard him gulping for air. The only thing separating

Norbert and myself from the cold touch of death was my ability to focus and put forth my best driving skills. Even at this speed, the bridge seemed long. Despite the pressure of the situation and other obstacles, the car never touched the sides. Then my foot was off the gas and soft on the brake. Nevertheless, when we passed the end of the bridge our speed was 75 mph. We risked so much by doing all this, and I am doubly glad there was no one else on the bridge.

What happened to the other dumb kids? I don't know, but I hope their car stopped before the river. They were locals, so some of the choices they made had to be based on knowledge of what lay ahead on the road. Getting out of that river valley and putting that part of the trip behind us felt good, even though we had done some things that should not have happened. Right or wrong, I threaded the needle at 90 mph.

We managed the remainder of the trip without getting into trouble and left the car in the Smythe's driveway all in good shape. We then made our way to my grandmother's small horse farm just outside of Amherst, where she had an extra room for us. My grandmother was now alone as my grandfather, Arthur Roth, had just died about a year earlier.

Now, regarding the second story of this trip, "Helen Roth's Respect for Norbert." My grandmother, Helen Roth, can give one the impression of a stern and not easily pleased person, the kind of person who would find fault with the world and the acts of people in it rathen than goodness and enjoyment. Correct or not, this is how I had always viewed Grandmother Helen Roth. So it was with some hesitation that I approached her, introducing Norbert Lopez. The first few minutes went as expected; but she must have heard something in the answers to her questions, something that gave her a good opinion of Norbert. It could have been his matter-of-fact way of speaking as he explained growing up on a 64,000-acre ranch where horses were used to round up cattle. Maybe the story of capturing wild horses on the ranch and breaking and training them for different ranchers in the area helped raise the value of his stock with Helen Roth. By the next day, after he walked the farm with her and showed her some of his skills with horses, she was smiling from ear to ear. I have never seen her so positive before. I heard everything they talked about and it sounded like everyday Norbert to me. I guess I never appreciated his skills and abilities until that day.

So, with this telling, a few more stories have become known. During the trip I had a lapse in judgment, but fate decided not to prosecute this time.

Ohio Trip 2005

THE NEXT TIME I VISITED AMHERST was in 2005. Faye and I stayed at a Holiday Inn Express in Vermillion, Ohio. We escorted my blind Aunt Sis from Phoenix to her 60th high school reunion. She was staying with her friend and classmate, Phyllis Darakis.

One overcast day we visited Crownhill Cemetery. The older stone markers are getting harder to read. Sis found some Thuemling graves. Yes, they are part of my bloodline. Thuemlings lived hard lives, according to the stories I've heard. Not all blood lines can achieve fame or fortune, and the Thuemlings made their share of mistakes.. Some or most are everyday people trying to make the best of some hard times. Sis found them by a big oak, which explained why so many acorns covered their graves. I thought to myself, Where are the squirrels?

Sis told us some of their sad stories. One marker read "Edwin Thuemling died at 19." We are told he worked on one of the ore boats. He had received his pay of $16 and was murdered for the money, which he was going to send home to his mother, Sophia.

I found some hundred-year-old sandstone mausoleums that stood guard on the edges of the hilltop cemetery, so old one had to think they had seen and kept their share of secrets. It seems like a world unto itself, on this hilltop surrounded by trees with not a house in sight. Faye was busy taking pictures, trying to capture the feel of Crownhill Cemetery so I might use the photos at a later date to produce paintings.

Pieces from the bloodline on my mother's side are found in another cemetery, St. Joseph's, which is down the road. These were under the names Menz and Plato. George Menz, born 1923, was a veteran of the Civil War, if the grave markers are to be believed. He might have met some of the people buried on Johnson Island in the Confederate prison cemetery. That was third cemetery we visited on our trip back to Ohio. The Johnson Island visit was with my aunt and uncle, Audrey and Don Starbuck. They took us, among other places, to Sandusky Bay and the surrounding area. They live in Wakeman, Ohio on some beautiful land that has given up some well-made Indian artifacts.

On the streets of Amherst I met a living distant cousin, Gerri Plato. She is now married to Dave Rice, who went to school with me. But is this Dave Rice from the high school class of 1963 or 1962? I have to find out. I have always thought there was an artistic gene in the Plato bloodline. From what I can discern of Gerri, the case of the artistic gene is strengthened. We found out about Gerri because of a park bench she borrowed from the village. The bench had painted on it "In memory of Paul Plato." Faye was taking a picture of it and someone asked if she knew Paul, and soon Gerri was there talking to us while I sat on the bench, much as Paul used to. And that is how one thing leads to another.

Also alive and well are Carson Plum and Larry Gates. The two fellows I grew up with until my fifteenth birthday. The summer I turned fifteen, my family moved to Arizona. So getting back to Amherst to talk to Carson and Larry filled in a lot of memory gaps. It was a lesson in how lives can take many paths.

All in all, I would say it was a good trip, and it is plain to see Amherst has grown and changed in many ways. In other ways, it has not changed at all. It has a sense of history both personal and social, and I am attracted to that. I am not much of a traveler, but I almost feel that I will be back. It could be that one does not return to their past. It is more like finding windows one can look through to view a particular image from the past.

Going back to Amherst I also find the town gives certain things to you, a place providing roots and so some acceptance. At the same time it demands knowledge of ones' personal life, thoughts and secrets. You learn in this exchange why you are the way you are, and maybe it does take a village to raise a child.

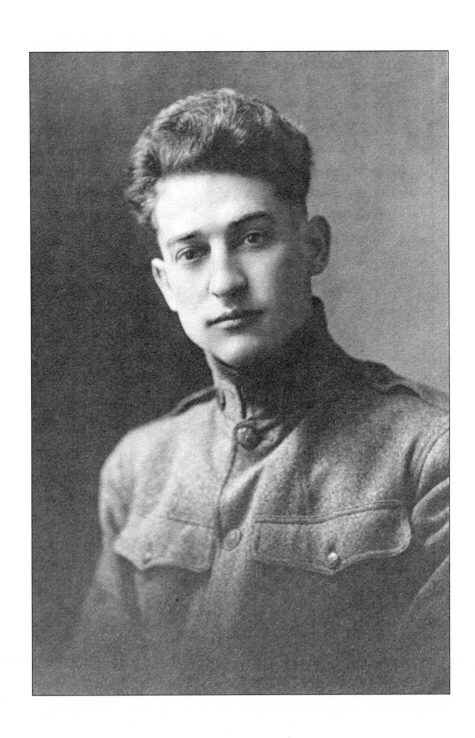

Grandfather's World War One Letters

ARTHUR P. ROTH WAS BORN in Lorain, Ohio on February 20, 1889. After high school he started work at the local steel mill, National Tube, and earned $4.40 per day. When he was twenty-eight, the United States entered the war in Europe. He enlisted in the Army Air Corps in August, 1917 and experienced World War I. Some of his basic training was in Ohio, but the more advanced training took place in Texas. His unit was then sent off to France, where he spent the rest of the war, allowing him to tour many French towns and cities. He sent many letters home, some of which I am making available to theany readers who would be interested in this sort of history.

Arthur Roth was my grandfather on my mother's side of the family. I always knew him as a good hard-working man. He was intelligent, modest, and had a good sense of humor. I believe parts of my life have been copied from his values and example.

The letter he wrote in 1919 was five pages long. The first page is missing, but as we pick it up on page two, it sounds as if he is touring France with some friends.

In the letter dated September 3, 1917 he is in San Antonio, Texas, the training base for the Army Air Corps. You might notice he is assigned to the 100th Aero Squadron. Also, the talk about food brands and cost gives us something to think about almost 100 years later.

In the letter dated April 11, 1919 he is stationed in Ourches Meuse, France. He spends a lot of time doing verbal games and fun with his younger sister, and note the reference to General Pershing.

In the letter dated May 11, 1919 he is in Le Mans, France and talks about how important sight-seeing is to him at this time.

So we get a glimpse of the thoughts and feelings of Arthur Roth during World War One. He seems very witty and skilled at writing with a great sense of humor.

WAR WORK COUNCIL
ARMY AND NAVY YOUNG MEN'S CHRISTIAN
ASSOCIATION
"WITH THE COLORS"

So. San Antonio, Texas,

Sept. 3, 1917.

Dear Mother, Dad and Sis:

How do you do. This is the great day called Labor Day, and such being the case we've no drills or work of any kind.

Things, such as ice cream, candy, towels, soap and practically anything of a household description which could be used here are way up in the air. I honestly believe they pull our legs. We have to pay 10¢ for a small bar of ice cream, about 3x2 inches. I mean, of course, at the Canteen or Company post exchange. Yesterday there were eight wagons at one end of the Camp, selling apples at 30¢ a dozen, ice cream cones reasonably at 5 cents each, pop at 5 cents and LaPearl (near beer) at 10 cents. They also sell water melons .at from 40 to 60 cents, depending how badly the fellows want them. If they won't pay 60 cents, why they let them have them for 50 or 40 cents. We have water melon every Sunday night.

We were out of quarantine yesterday, that means, that in a few days we will be able to get passes to town, and San Antonio, about 100,000 population, should be a city worth while seeing. The first thing the fellows will do probably will be getting a first-class feed.

I understand from your letter that you sent Sears, Roebuck & Co the $1.07, account additional price of material. You will, of course, keep yourself square with me, by deducting this amount from our account in the bank. And I thank you for looking after this matter so promptly.

I am not flying in the air. I am clerking so far. In order for one to fly, he must undergo a thorough examination (See the several last issues of the Saturday Evening post).

If one passes the examination, he is either sent to school for three months or has the equivalent in actual ground work. A man must be almost perfect in order to get a commission to fly. So don't worry. I do however, think that I am about as perfect as the next man, mind I am not bragging, but I came from healthy parents, and have had no diseases, for which I am thankful.

By being out of quarantine, we will soon move over to the Barracks (wooden long buildings) where we will remain for several weeks, maybe only a few days, but this will not change my address. We move from here to another training ground, there are several, and of course, we do not know which one as yet.

Lovingly yours,

Art

It has a population of 1900, not very big, but a large summer resort as evidenced by the many hotels. This undoubtedly is a wonderful place in the summer, but at this time of the year it had a blanket of snow of about four inches. We took several trips up the mountains and the distance is very deceiving to the eye. From the tops one gets a wonderful view of the country for many miles. In one instance it took us one hour to climb a more or less of a hill, and coming back by way of the tramway, we made it in fifteen minutes. The tramway was not operating and as the track was very steep and covered with snow we found our bodies made nice sleds, as in slipping and falling, our feet were not on the track one fifth of the time. We also visited Mont Dore seven kilos distant and found it on an order of La Bourboule only to our minds much better. This place is 3500 feet above sea level and this is manifested by the presence of a great deal more snow and also by the climate. We also found that we could get ice cream here, which you know as well without telling that we sampled, for the nominal sum of three francs or approximately sixty cents. This is, of course, a negligible sum for a soldier, especially on leave. What? One of the nice features here is a large building in the heart of the city devoted entirely to sulphur baths. On the way hack to La Bourboule, which by the way we walked, being down hill, we stopped at a petrifying fountain and enjoyed it very much. Annlmals, carvings on wood, fruits etc. are put under the falls and thereby are petrified. Besides seeing them in the process of petrification we also saw many of the finished products which were tres bon. Our hotel was jake. A regular bed and fine feeds. The French serve everything in courses even to a piece of cheese as small as your fingernail. We were at this area about five days, and while there was always something doing at the Y, the weather was quite cold, so we decided to make a run for it down south and see what we could see. Our leave here was for seven days, but on account of arriving at 9 AM, that day did not count, that is, our time started at midnight that day. So you see we had practically three days of our leave and four days journey to bank on, or in other words, seven days. We sallied forth passing through Ussel and Tulle and stopping for a few hours layover at Brive where we had a fine supper. Our next stop at Toulouse occasioned a long drive going through Cahors and Montauban. Here is where we got our first jolt vith the MPs if you can call this a jolt. They would not let us out of the station to get a bed. You see Toulouse is quite a place and many mademoiselles reside here and several soldiers heretofor going through went AWOL. We arrived here about 11 AM. We finally did persuade them to try several hotels in the immediate vicinity of the station, but they were all filled up. The sign "Complete" was conspicious in every one. There were many hotels in the main part of the town, a mile and a half distant, but Mr. MP would take no chances. We therefore had to go back to the station and make the best of it until 7 o'clock. It's a tough job waiting around a cold station take it from me. Our next stop was the walled city of Carcassonne at which place we arrived at 11 AM. We had about four hours to stay here as our next train for the first big and real stop at Montpellier was due at 3 PM!. First of all we had a real drink of cognac. This was the real stuff, stronger than any we had had hitherto. We had had some J & H Martell made in 1909 and thought this was good, but this stuff had it all over the other. We took in every thing Carcassonne offered, had a fine dinner and parted for Montpellier. The ride from Agde to Cette is a beauty, as the ride is between the Et de Thau and the Gulf. At Cette we changed trains without delay getting on the Express. We had a delightful time at Montpellier but had some time before getting a room. We arrived here about 7 PM and took in a good show after partaking of a fine feed at the hotel. Here there were several mademoiselles who could not make their eyes behave. We had until 4 o'clock the next afternoon to take in the city which I'll say we did. There were very few Americans here. We next hit the trail for Marseille passing through Nimes, transferring at Tarascon and going through Aries. We arrived at Marseille at night about 10 o'clock. We were lucky in getting a room the first shot, and again that welcome feed was had before retiring. Marsellle is surely a lovely place. It was here we first noticed the warmer temperature. In part I suppose to the fact that tables at many cafes and restaurants were out of doors. We had a wonderful ride via trolley on the high and rocky coast and saw some wonderful scenery. We also secured a tram ride to a high point visiting a large cathedral. From this point we could get a fine bird's eye view of the city. There are many soldiers here and we therefor got beaucoup cigarettes and candy and necessaries at the Y. We ledt Marseille for Nice at 2 PM on the Express arriving there about 9 PM. The ride to Nice is wonderful in view of the fact that at this time the moon was in full stew and shown [sic] out across the waters for our especial benefit. On the other side of the train we could see many things green, palms, ferns, rubber trees and tall pines. We noticed this particularly at Cannes. This is a beautiful place and we immediately had visions galore of what Nice would be like. At Nice we really had a hard time getting rooms. Two of the fellows got rooms prompto, but four of us sought for an hour before we got rooms, but they were very good and in the heart of the city. The next morning we got up early before the sun and journeyed via trolley to Monaco and Monte Carlo. This ride is entirely along the Mediterranean and as the moon had lighted the way for us the night previous, so the sun greeted us across the horizon. This ride was under the jurisdiction of the YMCA and we had two of their men with us. Our first stop was at Monte Carlo. We had left Nice at 6 AM and arrived at Monte Carlo at 8. We passed through some very fine country. Saw many orchards of olives, besides continually passing gardens of vegetables and flower beds. There was always that ever presence of oranges, lemons, ferns, large rubber trees, tall and stately pines and many clonging vines. Each villa we passed seemes possessed in abundance not alone in things green, but in architecture. One never sees wooden homes, but they are of the finest rock, not alone on the frontage, but the house complete. As a matter of fact there is an abundance of rock in France and Italy. Do not know of other countries adjoining, but would presume they have it also. The casino at Monte Carlo is only a few minutes from our stop. We had to wait until 8:30 before we vould go through it under guard. This time was easily spent in looking over the city, especially the park in front of the casino. It is very pretty. They have every so many trees and plants from all over the world. Each one has a tag showing from whence it came. To the left, or rather northeast of the casino is the Hotel de Paris operated as is the Cafe de Paris by the same corporation as operates the casino. The casino is very large and spacious. There are many paintings and works of art inside, as well as, well – you know roulette wheels etc. The ceiling is covered with a sort of bronze work of art. The walls in many places are covered with some very fine paintings, while the pillars are finely carved in every detail. It is very beautiful. The Prince of Monaco lents this out every year to a corporation for the sum of $250,000.00. The Corporation is incorporated for the sum of $6,000,000.00 and they have a rule that they never are to loose [sic] $250,000.00 in one days playing. Perhaps you remember a few years ago when they stopped playing one day from this cause. underground passage ways lead to the Hotel de Paris a few hundred feet distant. The Casino is on the sea front but faces the park. A large promenade at the rear of the Casino affords one a fine view of the sea. A few hundred feet to the rear of the Hotel de Paris is the baths operated by the same Corporation. This too is a fine sight. As you enter the building the first thing you see is a fine painting of the maidens taking a bath. The doorway is usually crowded, why? O Fie! The painting is a beauty and one just lingers, sort of risking one eye. One never tires of the works of architecture and paintings and this building like its sisters was a welcome to us. On one floor they have a room for sulphur baths of various temperatures, massaging and such other treatments to drive the poison from the body. Another floor had various instruments to improve the body, reduce superfluous flesh etc. The building on the whole was very extensive and worth seeing. At 9:30 we journeyed to Monaco and gave it the once over. The Prince of Monaco at this time was in Paris, so did not see him. We saw his palace however. During his absence there is one guard at the door, and when he is present, there are two. We went through the large cathedral after which we went through the musium [sic] which is made up entirely of specimens secured by the Prince. He is a great lover of the sea and has written many books on his travels. He is about sixty years old. The musium [sic] is very good. Monaco is located on a steep hill as is Monte Carlo, rather I should say the district of Monte Carlo. Between these two places is a small bay where we saw the Prince's yacht at anchor. At the bay between the two hills is a small business section. As I understand it, it is all known as Monaco. Before I forget it, the Prince requires the Corporation of the Casino of Monte Carlo to borrow large sums of money from him at a good rate of interest. How and why, I do not know. The people of Monaco do not pay any taxes, but are prohibited from gambling at the Casino. The people were not obligated to offer their services in the great war, but many did. In the business district at the bay we saw large rubber trees in front of the side walks about the size of our poplars. We had our dinner in the open by this bay. From Monaco we journeyed back to Monte Carlo at 1:30 to catch our streetcar and journey to Menton and thence over the border into Italy. Before I forget it, all of the coast towns are backed by large hills. These hills start their climb in many cases almost from the sea, and as a consequence many of the houses are some distance from the bottom. It seemed funny to us to have to climb that far up hill to go to and from town, but I suppose it would be natural to us if we had always lived there. Our track, as before stated, ran in the main on the high cliffs overlooking the sea and many times we went through tunnels, sometimes made with just the excavation of the rock. Our Y man pointed out many castles and fortifications on top of the hills which at one time figured prominently in the history of the world. Menton is not very large, but like all other cities in this locality is very beautiful. We had a few hours stop here and journeyed over the border. At the border line were signorittas with their wares, chiefly postal cards and some water color paintings. As we know that salt is salt, so we knew at a glance that these were Italian pictures; it was such a striking contrast, especially at this point in tne world. We would have journeyed to Vintimille, but an MP in the road would not let us go. He was stationed about a kilometer from the border. We had a fine day of it and got back to our hotel about six o'clock, having missed our 1:30 train. (We missed it on purpose.) We were to get the 7:30 out the next morning. We spent an enjoyable evening looking over the city and journeying to the Y. The Y at night looks like a glass palace standing out over the sea. This casino is directly off of a large and beautiful park just a few minutes from our hotel, "Balmoral." The Y is packed every evening with soldiers and we also saw many Red Cross Nurses on leave.

Dancing is from 10 to 12. Nice seemed live and active in the fact that the cafes and restaurants were wide open until midnight, quite different from other places. We left Nice the next morning at 8 o'clock on the Express arriving in Marseille at seven. We had a layover of four hours and so had plenty of time to get a good feed and restock on cigarettes and other necessities. We got the 11 o'clock Express for Paris and had a long and tiring ride of 23 hours. All through our trip the cars were packed to the limit. Sometimes we rode third class, sometimes second and again first class, all depending on the fullness of the cars. We were privileged to ride second class, but not first. So matter what class we rode we always found the Frenchman in large numbers with us, but he was continually criticising us for riding his cars and taking up the room. This had been the case ever since leaving Toul and it gradually got worse as we traveled. We probably were good comrades while in the trenches, but on riding trains he has no earthly use for us. By the way on all of our trips we never saw a sleeper. I don't say they have not got them, but apparently this seems the case. On our way to Paris we passed through some large cities as Arles, Tarascon, Avignon, Orange, Montelimar, Valance, Vienne, the large railroad center of Lyon, Macon, Chalon, again hit Dijon, Tonnerre, Joigny, Sens, Melun, and Corbeil. We arrived at Paris at 9 o'clock at night and were supposed to leave at 7:30 the next morning, but after seeing the Provost Marshall and presenting our pleas of a long and tiring ride, he finally extended our time to noon. Paris at this time of the night was as tight as a drum, quite a contrast as compared with Nice. We met a pal who took us over the city at this hour in search of a feed and a place to bunk for the night. He knew the subways like a book and we made good time, but it was fully an hour before we got a bite to eat at a Red Cross Canteen. We bunked for the night at a Red Cross Hut and had a fine breakfast in the morning about 7.50. We therefor had from 8 to 12 to see as much of the city as possible and make our train. Again we were lucky meeting a Y man with idle time on his hands, who proceeded to take us around as much as possible. We previously had however visited Napoleon's Tomb, but did not see it, as it had bean walled and covered with sandbags as a protection from air raids. They were working on the job of uncovering it. We had also seen the Magdalene Cathedral which was very good. The Y man took us to the Touleurs Gardens in which there are many things of interest. We saw the Arc of Triump and the many inscriptions of the names of great men and battles and the meaning therefor, as they had all done great things for France or had beau big battles in the Nation's history. Undoubtedly Pres. Wilson's name will be added. The marching under the Arc of Triump is a great honor and courtesy. Possibly you remember this was the Kaiser's intention in the summer of 1918 when he was so close and yet so far from this great city. We saw the statues of France's provinces, noticing particularly that that of Strasbourg was now uncovered. It had been covered for four years as a sign of mourning for her. We saw the Palace de Glace, where many of the big athletic events in Paris are being held. We saw the Eifel Tower from a distance. We could not get closer than a block to it. It was carefully guarded. In many of the streets we saw captured cannon in great numbers, and of many types and sizes. We saw the palace where Marie Antoinette and her Court held sway and the Courtyard adjoining. Unlike many other cities in France, Paris was laid out in building. This is evidenced by the large and spacious boulevards. Their subway is great. We would have liked to have seen much more of Paris and also seen Versailles, but four hours is so often a very short length of time. In journeying from Paris to Toul, practically the end of our journey, we passed through Meaux, Chateau Thierry, Epernay, Chalons, Vitry, Bar-Le-Duc and Commercy. Chateau Thierry as far as we could see was practically unharmed, but the villages east of it surely got it. Some were a pile of stone and brick, some with the buildings half demolished and practically useless. We could see where bridges had been blown away and others out in their places. Some buildings were full of holes, large and small. This reminds one of the destruction of Thiacourt and Verdun and many other villages in aud around this vicinity. Our ride from Paris to Toul took eight hours. We arrived in Toul at 8 PM and had one sweet job finsing a bunk for the night. The Y had rooms but would not give them to us unless ee had an order from the RTO. A fine thing. All the hotels were filled up. We finally spied the KC and got some fine bods, and altho we were almost home, knew there would be no reveille in the morning. The next morning about 9 bells we got up and the KC gave us a fine breakfast. We then journeyed to Air Service Headquarters & caught one of our trucks which makes a daily trip to this place, and picks up Officers and men from leave or duty. It sure seemed great in a way to get back after our long trip. But it was cold, yes very cold. Imagine jumping from Nice of sunshine and flowers to the very opposite. We had this cold spell for about three weeks before it finally thawed, we now have that rain and mud as in days of yore. The people here say the winter is over; it must be, for it sure rains enough to make up for lost time. And the Princess and Prince lived happily ever after.

The mention of wine, cognac and women is not given with the intention of giving you the impression that we indulged wildly in exotic pleasure in this pastime. Not at all. Of course, we had drinks, but not many; we were out for sight seeing, not for a stew party, besides this was not practicable, as we were in a territory not called for on our passes. In the small towns one does not see much of mademoiselle; it is usually old men and women, but in the towns we passed through, mademoiselle was just as much a butterfly (not poor butterfly) as in any other part of the globe. I sent four packages of cards; you write of only receiving two. Trust the rest will come along in good season. Have been some time getting to this letter, but better late than never. Have no definate [sic] news of leaving as yet. Best wishes to all.

Lovingly,
Art

Corp Arthur P Roth,
100th Aero Sqdn.,
Amer EF, France.

KNIGHTS OF COLUMBUS
WAR ACTIVITIES

Ourches, Meuse, France
April 11, 1919.

Dear tres jollie Mademoiselle Petite a la Carte de Luxe:

Greeting Oh Sister of mine. How be you. Bein' as how I done received your most interesting letter, (illustrated) and written in a hand as light as my lady's heart, why— Oh shucks I sorta pledged meself to sit me down and chat with thee, just like that. This machine has got the Saint Fittas Dance, so look out for Jimme Dale. He'll get you with the green seal no matter where you sit, not set. Sitting reminds me of hens. A pal of mine said the other day that where he came from it was so hot they had to give their chickens cracked ice, but this even did not help matters; the hens in spite of it, laid hard boiled eggs. How's that. You know me Al; I never explain my own jokes. Far be it from sich. But, bein'as how you be a school teacher (pardon the captials) you be educated in the ways of the jokes of the King's Fool. So much for an overture.

Today we passed in review before General Pershing and listend to a fine speech by him afterwards. We arrived at the field at 10 AM and partied at 4 PM. Of course, there was some time utilized in getting the many units in their proper position, but we did wait a long time for old John to gaze into the crystal of the Yogi (our blue and brown eyes that never lie) and learn where of we were faultless in our attire, which was not visible to the naked eye, unless Jimmie Dale was in attendence. Dost follow me, thou who hast been decorated with the XYZ. Fie Mademoiselle, perchance thou would'st look beneath me, but I'll fix that; a box of bon bons will do the trick.

Litte Dame Runor has been busy again with her sewing bee news. She says as how we are to partie toot sweet for the land of [indecipherable]. It sorta looks as how she done quit scoutin' duty and ventured within the lines with valuable information.

I done wanna bring back a mademoiselle Francaise, 'cause you and her could never get along nohow. She'd be calling you names and you'd be calling her names incognito, and that would never do. And Dad might think both of you were planning to ruin his lettuce bed and what not. Anyhow she'd insist on having the manure pile in the front yard, and this would never do. Again she'd insist on putting blinds on all the windows and closing them as soon as the lights were lit, and people passing along on the street would a think t'was an empty lot, and this would never do. Comprenez vous? And again --------- oh what's the use, she's so different, so vastly different in so many things. I mean the girl in the small cities, different in everything but her smile, and women the world over always did belie a man into thinking black was white. Huh! Ask Mother! Pinch yourself. Tee Hee. You see I'm safe over here. I should worry. Listen, you never acknowledged receipt of that precious gift in the usual formal manner. I'm surprised at your lack of etiquette, especially a School Teacher.

No more; I might commit myself. Oh yes. I hope that new Easter gown you are going to wear will be the envy of all the girls that gaze thereat and the gentlemen of Arts Classe. This is the stuff you like. Huh?

Best wishes.

Lovingly,

Art

This rumor has been confirmd with an order and we leave in a few days for Colombey Les Belles for Demobolization, which I understand will be soon, possibly within one or two weeks.

Le Mans, France,
May 11, 1919.

Dear Mother,

This is Mother's Day and naturally you will expect a letter from me in commemoration of not only the day, but of your honorable self. C'nest nes pas. Huh? But, I will beat this letter home. See. What you call "Ginger." This is an embarkation camp. We have been here since the 5th. We had a preliminary field inspection this AM and tomorrow have our final. Expect to leave Tuesday for either St. Nazaire or Brest. The 6th I recd. one of your letters stating the Harry Beatty was in the 12th Aero. He was at Colombey with us and came on the same train for this place. We have not corresponded. I could not because he was in the casuals when I first met him and did not know to what outfit he was finally assigned. Looked him up here and had a fine chat together. Bube writes of going to Germany soon, but expecting a pass for Paris and also to Nice, of which I unfolded the wonders of that place. Just like that. Received a letter today from Howard, written at Cuba. However he stated that he expected to be sent to New York to take part in the big pageant and later go to Phila for three months. He is very hard on the naval life and desires to get out of it the worst way. However I don't see what can be done. Of course it can be done when one has good influence. Visited Le Mans proper last night on a six hour pass. It is some place believe me. Got a book of the places of interest. This is my fad. Alo got a book of the cathedrals in Eurpoe which is jake, also one of Metz which is the only place of the cards I have sent you, that I have not been. No, I am not bragging. If we really do leave now, I will not write from this side again, see.

Let me say that I am sending my best compliments on your 23rd wedding anniversary, which, according to the records of my secretary is the 16th of this month. Just think is it not remarkable that the Roths never quarreled, never wrangled, never fought like two dying cats, never cared how late the other stayed out 'o nights and everything. Tat's what they tell you when one has a blow out, only people blow up ------- with pride and everything.

I did not send Margaret a birthday card, because girls are so particular about ages, especially taking sixteen for anything else of higher denomination. A fine thing, as the King said.

Best wishes to all,
Art

Fred Taylor was born in Portsmouth, Virginia in 1945 and grew up in Amherst, Ohio. He served five years in the Navy, with the last two years with MCB5 in Danang and Dong Ha, Vietnam. Fred married Fay Saito in 1971 and graduated from UCSB in 1973. They moved to Madison, Wisconsin and lived on a farm for twenty-eight years. In 1997 Fred was diagnosed with Parkinson's disease and currently lives in SaddleBrooke, Arizona. He can be reached by writing to 38404 S. Apache Peak Drive, Tucson AZ 85739 or phoning 520-825-0187.

CPSIA information can be obtained
at www.ICGtesting.com
Printed in the USA
FSOW02n1923021215
13724FS

9 781935 437871